W9-BAY-067

Mother Goose's Animal Farm

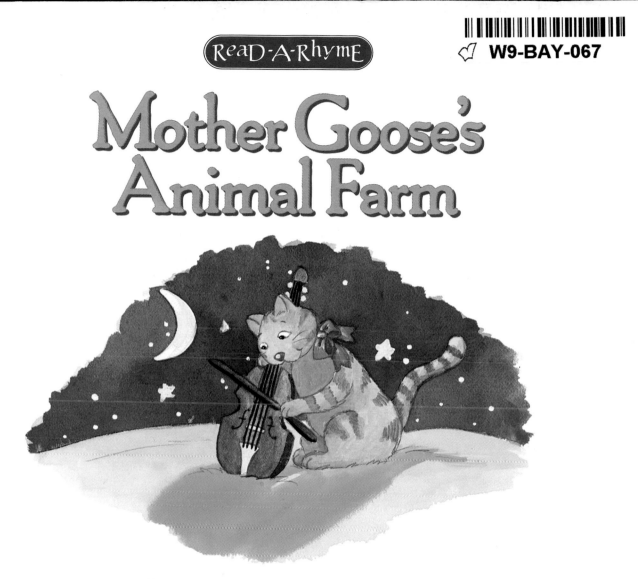

Illustrated by Tammie Speer-Lyon

2 4 6 8 10 9 7 5 3

Modern Publishing
A Division of Unisystems, Inc.
New York, New York 10022
Series UPC #19585

Old Mother Goose,
When she wanted to wander,
Would ride through the air
On a very fine gander.

Little Miss Muffet
Sat on a tuffet,
Eating her curds and whey.

Along came a spider
And sat down beside her,
And frightened Miss Muffet away.

Three little kittens, they lost their mittens,
And they began to cry,
"Oh, Mother dear, we sadly fear
That we have lost our mittens!"
"What, lost your mittens?
You naughty kittens!
Then you shall have no pie!"
"Mee-ow, mee-ow, mee-ow."
"No, you shall have no pie."

The three little kittens, they found their mittens,
And they began to cry,
"Oh, Mother dear, see here, see here,
For we have found our mittens!"
"Put on your mittens, you silly kittens,
And you shall have some pie."
"Purr-r, purr-r, purr-r!
Oh, let us have some pie."

The three little kittens put on their mittens,
And soon ate up the pie.
"Oh, Mother dear, we greatly fear
That we have soiled our mittens."
"What, soiled your mittens?
  You naughty kittens!"
  Then they began to sigh,
    "Mee-ow, mee-ow, mee-ow!"
  Then they began to sigh.

The three little kittens, they washed their mittens,
And hung them out to dry.
"Oh, Mother dear, do you not hear
That we have washed our mittens?"
"What, washed your mittens?
Then you're good kittens.
But I smell a rat close by."
'Mee-ow, mee-ow, mee-ow!
We smell a rat close by."

Hickety, pickety, my black hen,
She lays eggs for gentlemen.
Gentlemen come every day
To see what my black hen doth lay.

Baa, baa, black sheep, have you any wool?
Yes, sir, yes, sir, three bags full.
One for my master and one for my dame,
And one for the little boy who lives down the lane.

I love little Pussy,
Her coat is so warm,
And if I don't hurt her,
She'll do me no harm.

So I'll not pull her tail,
Nor drive her away;
But Pussy and I
Very gently will play.

Goosey, goosey, gander,
Whither shall I wander?
Upstairs and downstairs
And in my lady's chamber.
There I met an old man
Who wouldn't say his prayers.
I took him by the left leg
And threw him down the stairs.

Little Bo-Peep has lost her sheep,
And can't tell where to find them.
Leave them alone, and they'll come home,
Wagging their tails behind them.

Little Bo-Peep fell fast asleep,
And dreamt she heard them bleating;
But when she awoke, she found it a joke,
For they were all still fleeting.

Then up she took her little crook,
Determined for to find them;
She found them indeed, but it made her heart bleed,
For they'd left all their tails behind them!

It happened one day, as Bo-Peep did stray
Into a meadow hard by,
There she espied their tails side by side,
All hung on a tree to dry.

She heaved a sigh and wiped her eye,
And over the hillocks she raced;
And tried what she could, as a shepherdess should,
That each tail should be properly placed.

A long-tailed pig and a short-tailed pig
Went to the garden to dance a jig.

They danced and danced, the garden 'round,
And knocked the flowers to the ground.

They jigged and jogged to Dover Town,
And turned the market upside-down.

H

iggledy, piggledy, pop!
The dog has swallowed the mop;

The pig's in a hurry;
The cat's in a flurry;
Higgledy, piggledy, pop!

Hey, diddle, diddle, the cat and the fiddle,
The cow jumped over the moon.
The little dog laughed to see such sport,
And the dish ran away with the spoon.

This little piggy
went to market.

This little piggy
stayed home.

This little piggy
had roast beef.

This little piggy
had none.

This little piggy cried, "Wee, wee, wee, wee,"
All the way home.

Ding, dong, bell,
Pussy's in the well!
Who threw her in?
Little Tommy Lin.

Who pulled her out?
Little Johnny Stout.
What a naughty boy was that
To try to drown poor pussy-cat,
Who never did him any harm,
But killed the mice in his father's barn.

P

ussy-cat, Pussy-cat,
Where have you been?
I've been to London,
To see the Queen.
Pussy-cat, Pussy-cat,
What did you there?
I frightened a little mouse
Under her chair.

Three blind mice; three blind mice!
See how they run; see how they run!
They all ran after the farmer's wife,
Who cut off their tails with a carving knife.
Did ever you see such a sight in your life
  as three blind mice?

Mary had a little lamb,
Whose fleece was white as snow;
And everywhere that Mary went,
The lamb was sure to go.

It followed her to school one day,
Which was against the rule.
It made the children laugh and play
To see a lamb at school.

And so the teacher turned it out,
But still it lingered near;
And waited patiently about,
Till Mary did appear.

"Why does the lamb love Mary so?"
The children all did cry.
"Why, Mary loves the lamb, you know,"
The teacher
did reply.

O nce I saw a little bird
Come hop, hop, hop,
And I cried, "Little bird,
Will you stop, stop, stop?"

I was going to the window
To say, "How do you do?"
But he shook his little tail
And away he flew.